PRIYA DREAMS of Marigolds & Masala

Written and Illustrated by

MEENAL PATEL

BEAVER'S POND PRESS

With love for

PRIYA BEAR & NEELA BUNNY

and

PARK BA & BUNNY BA

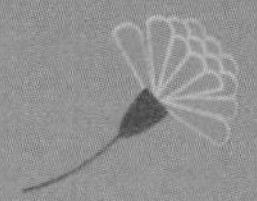

THIS HOUSE IS ON A SMALL STREET IN A SMALL CITY IN THE UNITED STATES.

It's the only house on the street with an Indian family.

It's the only house on the street that has a garland of bright orange marigolds hanging in the doorway.

It's the only house on the street with a family inside who passes around rotli for dinner.

It's the only house on the street where an old woman emerges in a colorful sari to pick marigolds from the garden.

Priya rushes into the house after school.
She hears the clang of metal pots and
smells simmering spices.

Babi Ba has already started cooking dinner, but she always waits for Priya to help her make rotli.

The kids at school didn't know what rotli was until Priya explained it's a type of flatbread from India. Babi Ba mixes the flour, water, and ghee to form a long rope of dough.

Priya pinches off little pieces and rolls them into balls between her palms. Babi Ba quickly rolls the balls out thin and round before cooking them on the stove and drizzling them with ghee. They do this together every day.

And every day Priya asks Babi Ba, “What is India like?”

Babi Ba tells her India is the smell of roasted cumin and the masala at the spice market that tickles your nose.

It's the sound of motorbikes whizzing by, mixed with the beep-beep of a tuk-tuk and the moo of a cow.

It's the arches and domes on buildings
and the grit of the streets.

It's the hot sun on your face and
the drenching monsoon rains.

It's the rainbow of saris stacked to the ceiling in a shop and the quiet swish-swish of a sari with every step.

It's the taste of a steaming cup of cha that the cha-wala hands you and the warmth of his smile.

It's the hustle and bustle of crowds of people going this way and that and the mix of beliefs and traditions they carry within them.

It's the marigolds strung up on the storefronts and the doorways of homes.

Priya asks, “Babi Ba, will you take me to India?”

Babi Ba replies, “Maybe one day we will be able to go there.”

Priya thinks for a moment. “Do you miss it?”

“Sometimes, yes. But then I remind myself that India is here in the marigolds from our garden and the smell of roasted cumin.”

“And the swish-swish of your sari,” Priya adds.

Babi Ba smiles. “India is with us in the things that we do every day.”

They sit down for dinner with the whole family and pass the rotli.

In the winter when it snows, Priya notices that Babi Ba doesn't go out in the morning because there are no marigolds to pick.

Priya wonders if this makes
Babi Ba miss India even more.

The next day at school Priya makes little orange marigolds out of paper during art class.

When the class crowds around to see what she is doing, she tells them about the marigolds and the masala and the beep-beep of the tuk-tuks.

One by one, they join in to make the longest garland of marigolds that Priya has ever seen.

Babi Ba's face lights up when she sees the garland of paper marigolds hung up in the doorway.

Priya says, "The kids at school were excited to hear about India and they helped me make this garland."

Babi Ba's smile grows even bigger.
She gathers Priya up in her arms and says,

"SHARING INDIA WITH OTHERS IS THE VERY BEST WAY TO CARRY IT WITH YOU."

HALFWAY ACROSS THE GLOBE IS A HOUSE ON A SMALL STREET IN A SMALL CITY IN GUJARAT, INDIA.

It's one of many houses on the street that has a garland of bright orange marigolds hanging in the doorway.

It's one of many houses on the street with a family inside who passes around rotli for dinner.

It's one of many houses on the street where an old woman emerges in a colorful sari to pick marigolds from the garden.

MEANINGS, DEFINITIONS, PRONUNCIATIONS

Elements in this book were influenced by life in Gujarat, but there are many different cultural traditions, religions, and languages within this state and throughout India. Some of the cultural practices, symbolism, and Gujarati words in this book may overlap with other regions and languages throughout India and South Asia.

Marigolds

These flowers are native to Mexico and Central America. They carry different meanings for cultures around the world.

The use of garlands and meanings of specific flowers vary throughout India and are used in ceremonies by different religions. In Gujarat and other regions, some people hang fresh marigold and mango leaf garlands at the entrance of homes, shops, and even on trucks for festive occasions. They are a symbol of honor and luck. They hang in doorways as a welcoming gesture for visitors.

The Hindi word for these garlands is *toran* (*toh*-run), which also refers to a decorated textile that is hung in doorways for the same purposes.

Ba (ba)

Gujarati word for *mom* or *grandmother* (as in this story). Many Gujarati people use Ma for grandmother but my family uses Ba.

Ghee (ghi)

Butter that has been simmered down to remove water and milk solids. People use ghee for cooking, as well as in religious ceremonies.

Cha (chah)

Known as *chai* in other parts of India and South Asia. The word refers generally to many kinds of tea but is often used in reference to a type of tea called *masala cha*, which is black tea brewed with spices and milk over a flame or stovetop.

Mandir (*mun*-deer)

A place of worship. In a Hindu home, it's where people keep images of deities and worship daily. They often have flowers in the mandir that are offerings to the deities.

Masala (*ma*-sa-lah)

General reference to a mix of spices. Some common spices that are mixed in various combinations include cumin, fennel, coriander, cardamom, and cayenne pepper.

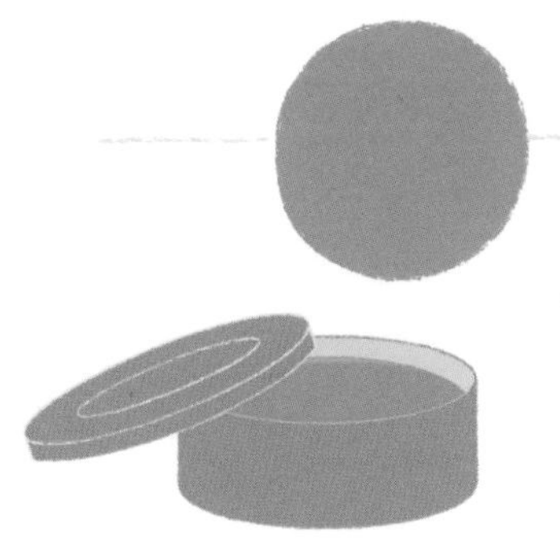

Rotli (*roht*-lee)

A very thin flatbread made from wheat flour. It is also known as *roti*, *chapati*, or *phulka* in other regions. It is a daily staple for lunch and dinner in some Gujarati households. You tear off a piece of rotli with your hands and use it to scoop up a bite of other foods (vegetable, lentil, or meat dishes).

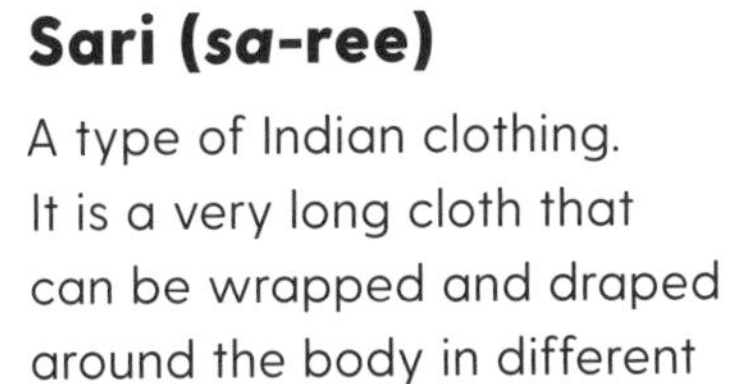

Sari (*sa*-ree)

A type of Indian clothing. It is a very long cloth that can be wrapped and draped around the body in different ways. There are many colors, patterns, and fabrics to choose from.

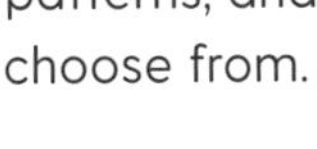

Tuk-Tuk (took-took)

A small three-wheeled motorized vehicle. Also known as a *rickshaw*. They are very common in India and are used similarly to a taxi cab.

Wala (*wa*-la)

Someone who sells a particular item. For example, in this story the cha-wala sells cha.

AUTHOR'S NOTE

I'm an Indian-American woman. I was born and raised in the United States but my family is from Gujarat, India. When I went to India as an adult, I was struck by how it was both foreign and familiar to me. Many things that were a part of my childhood home growing up felt so different from others in the United States but turned out to be so common in India.

I kept seeing marigold garlands strung up and it reminded me of my Ba. When she lived with us in the United States, she would pick marigolds from our garden every morning to put in our mandir. I recognized the abundance of marigolds in India as a beautiful piece of my family's identity that we carried in our everyday lives. There were so many things like this—mandirs, images of familiar gods and goddesses, the rustling of saris, the smell of cha. All of these things that made me feel different in the United States were unnecessary to explain in India. They were a part of everyday life.

I had a wonderful life as a child but I put up walls between all of my identities because I was afraid of being different. It wasn't until I was an adult that I realized how important it is to allow all parts of my identity to mix, to share all parts of me with people. I hope this book inspires kids to take pride in all their identities—all the unique threads that come together to make them who they are. I hope it inspires them to share their own unique cultures and to be curious about other cultures.

Learn more at

WWW.MEENALPATELSTUDIO.COM

ISBN: 978-1-64343-955-6
Library of Congress Catalog Number: 2019930793
Printed in the United States of America
First Printing: 2019
23 22 21 20 19 5 4 3 2 1

Edited by Lily Coyle and Hanna Kjeldbjerg
Cover and interior design by Meenal Patel

Beaver's Pond Press, Inc.
7108 Ohms Lane
Edina, MN 55439–2129
(952) 829-8818
www.BeaversPondPress.com

To order, visit www.ItascaBooks.com
or call (800) 901-3480.
Reseller discounts available.